THE TALKING MICKEY MOUSE SHOW

The City Beneath the Sand

W•W
WORLDS OF WONDER™

Printed in U.S.A. / P35   ISBN: 1-55578-303-1

Mickey   Aren't museums fun places to visit? They're full of strange, wonderful and beautiful things. On this particular trip to the museum Goofy, Pluto and I were even more excited than usual.

Goofy   We'd come to answer a call from our old buddy, Professor Bing.

Bing   Welcome, boys. I'm glad you could make it. I believe you already know my assistant, Lurk.

Goofy   Yup, last time we visited he showed us the new exhibits.

Lurk   It's good to see you again, fellows, but you'll have to excuse me. The professor wants me to take these reports down to our lab.

Goofy   So long, Lurk. We'll be seein' you.

Mickey   After Lurk left, the professor closed the door and pulled a map out onto his desk.

Bing   Boys, the shifting sands of the Sahara Desert have recently uncovered the ancient city of Kichikoochi.

Goofy   Gawrsh!

Bing   The museum would like you to go there and bring back pictures and relics for us.

Mickey   Aren't you going to send your assistant, Lurk?

Bing   I'm afraid not. On our last expedition he tried to keep some of the relics for himself.

Goofy   Hey look, Mick, Pluto's barkin' at the door. Aren't dogs funny sometimes?

Mickey   Quiet, Pluto. This is a museum. Are there any other instructions, Professor?

Bing   No, we'll arrange for everything—transportation, equipment, and guides. Can you do it, boys?

Mickey   We'll be ready tomorrow!

Goofy   Yup. An' raring to go!

Mickey In a few days, Goofy and I were making our way deep into the Sahara Desert.

Goofy Hey Mick, are those trees up ahead or one of those garages?

Mickey You mean *mirages*?

Goofy Oh, yeah.

Mickey That's no mirage, Goofy. It's the oasis of Hogwallah, where we pick up our guide.

Goofy   That must be him now—the big fella with the beard.

Ben   Mr. Mouse, Mr. Goofs, and Pluto! I am expecting you! My name is Ben Ahrownd.

Mickey   Glad to meet you, Mr. Ahrownd. Professor Bing said you're the best guide in these parts.

Ben   Is true. We go now and I will lead you to the ancient city of Kichikoochi.

Mickey   Ben took us on an old caravan route. Goofy didn't like it too much.

Goofy   Whoa, this is a bumpy ride!

Ben   Yes, trail is hard for truck. Camels would be better. But city is not far now.

Mickey   Look, Ben, on the trail ahead of us. There are some people blocking our way.

Goofy   And they don't look very happy!

Ben   Don't worry, my friends. They are the Doowahdiddi people. They live near here. I talk to them.

Mickey	Goofy and I got pretty nervous while we waited.
Goofy	Gawrsh, I wonder what they're sayin'. Uh-oh, he's coming back.
Ben	Mick, Goofs, all is okay. They know where city is. They show us exact spot if you give them some food.
Goofy	It's a deal. Maybe they're friendly after all.
Mickey	Pluto sure doesn't think so.

Goofy   The Doowahdiddies took us to a narrow pass. Then all of a sudden they stopped!

Ben   Mickey and Goofs, they say city very close, just through this pass, but they go no further. To walk in ancient city is bad luck. We leave truck here to make camp.

Mickey   Okay, Ben, let's give them the food we promised.

Goofy   Gawrsh, these guys sure are hungry. Look, Mick, they're sharin' some of it with Pluto. That's enough to make him friends with anybody!

Goofy   Mickey, Pluto, Ben and I hiked through the pass.

Mickey   Ben, I was hoping we might get the natives to help us dig. Maybe you can convince them there's no reason to worry about bad luck.

Ben   First got to convince self!

Goofy   Look, Mick, up ahead—that must be it!

Mickey   The ancient city of Kichikoochi! Come on, fellows, let's have a look around.

Goofy   Hey, Mick, Pluto's bringing one of his bones right into the ruins!

Mickey   That's right, Pluto, we're here to dig. But we want to uncover treasures, not bury them.

Goofy   Wait a minute, he stopped diggin'. Why's his head cocked like that? It's almost like he's listenin' to somethin'.

Mickey   Goofy, that column next to you is starting to fall! Look out!

Goofy   Whoa! Gawrsh, Mick, I guess I moved just in the nick of time.

Ben   It is warning, Goofs. To walk in city is bad luck.

Mickey   I don't think so, Ben. That column was thousands of years old. It was bound to fall sooner or later. I'd say we were pretty lucky to spot it in time to warn Goofy.

Ben   Maybe so, maybe no. But is getting late. City may be dangerous. We go back to truck now and make camp.

Mickey	The next morning, Pluto's barking woke us up.
Goofy	What's that rumbling sound, Mick?
Mickey	I'll poke my head outside the tent to see. It's a boulder! Let's get out of here!
Goofy	Gawrsh, that was close! It squashed the tent flat!
Ben	Mick, Goofs, I am coming. Are you okay?
Mickey	Yes, Pluto warned us of the danger just in time. Where were you, Ben?
Ben	I always go on early morning walk.
Mickey	Well, let's pack up our equipment and head for the city.

Mickey   At the edge of the city, Goofy and I pulled out our shovels to start digging.

Goofy   Gawrsh, this is excitin'. No tellin' what we'll find. Where's your shovel, Ben?

Ben   I no go in city. We already have more bad luck this morning. But whatever you dig up I will carry back to camp for you.

Mickey All day long we dug up treasure after treasure—pottery, coins, jewelry, all kinds of things. Ben carried them back to camp to pack into the truck.

Goofy You know, Mick, it's funny. Ben's the one who's worried about bad luck, but he's always a lucky distance away when somethin' unlucky happens.

Mickey Maybe this bad luck legend was started by someone who didn't want anyone to visit the city.

Mickey   When we got back to camp, Goofy couldn't resist going to the truck to see all the treasures one more time.

Goofy   Gawrsh! Mick, Ben, come quick!

Mickey   Oh, my gosh, the truck is empty! Where is everything, Ben?

Ben   I don't know. Ben leaves it all right here. There must be thieves about. Is more bad luck.

Mickey
Goofy Come sunrise, Goofy woke up first and looked around. Boy, that ol' sun's hot already. Say, there's a pond over yonder. Funny I didn't notice it before. I wonder if that's where Ben goes on his mornin' walks? I'll let Mick and Pluto sleep a little longer while I take a little dip an' cool off.

Goofy   Gawrsh, this place is a lot further off than I thought. Hey, it's disappearing! It must be one of them mee-rages. I better go back before I get lost.

Mickey   Goofy tried to follow his footprints back, but the wind had filled them with sand.

Goofy   Wow, I can't even see for the dust. I better shut my eyes. I have a pretty good sense of direction.

Mickey   Back at camp, I decided not to dig in the city. It was too windy to work safely. Besides, I was worried about Goofy.

Mickey   Meanwhile Goofy kept wandering around with his hands over his eyes. Finally, the wind died down.

Goofy   Maybe it's safe to open my eyes now. Yeow! I'm on the edge of a cliff! Boy, my sense of direction sure needs overhaulin'. I wonder where I am?

Mickey   Goofy looked around and saw a campsite.
Goofy   There's nobody here. Gawrsh, would you look at this funny-lookin' gadget. Here's the power switch. Huh, it lights up, but it doesn't do anythin'. Oh, well, I'm bushed. Maybe I should take a little nap until things blow over.

Goofy	While I was sleeping, Mickey was back at camp. He heard loud noises coming from the city.
Mickey	Come on, Ben, let's see what's up.
Ben	No, city is too dangerous. I am afraid—too much bad luck.
Mickey	Then Pluto and I are going. Come on, Pluto. Why are you barking so much? Over there? But Pluto, the city's this way. Okay, okay, I'll follow you.

Mickey   Gee, Pluto, it's a campsite. So this is what you were barking at—a machine, with the switch turned on.

Goofy   Hi, Mick.

Mickey   Goofy! What are you doing here?

Goofy   I was havin' a nap in this camp when Pluto's barkin' woke me up.

Mickey   I've got a hunch, Goof. Let's switch off this machine.

Goofy   That's funny, Pluto stopped barkin'.

Mickey   It must give off a sound that Pluto can hear but we can't. I'll bet this is someone's secret camp. And I think I know who that someone might be.

Mickey Come on, Goof, let's head back to the city. There were some awful sounds coming from that direction.

Goofy Uh-oh, here comes the wind again. Gawrsh, Mick, it's hard to see but it looks like a lot of the old buildings toppled over.

Mickey Someone's creeping along the side of that big building. Maybe it's our mysterious camper. If we sneak up, maybe we can get the drop on him.

Goofy Okay, mister, stop right there! Ben, it's you!

Ben Pluto, Mick, Goofs, you are safe! I am glad. Come, I have something to show you.

Mickey Sorry, Ben, it's not going to work. We saw your camp.
Ben Camp? Please just follow.
Goofy Be careful, Mick. It could be a trick.
Mickey Wait, I can see something. It looks like a man tied up to one of the columns!
Ben When the noises from the city stop, I hear cries for help. I think you were in trouble, so I forget my fear and run into city. But instead of you, I find this stranger trapped in caved-in building. I think he is thief who rob your truck yesterday.
Goofy Gawrsh, it's Lurk!

Lurk   That's right. That day at the Professor's office, I was listening outside the door.

Mickey   So that's why Pluto was barking!

Lurk   Right again. Then he got in the way every time I turned on my sound machine out here. No one else could hear the soundwaves that caused things to vibrate and fall.

Goofy   Then you must have been the one who robbed our truck.

Lurk   Yes, and when none of you came to the city today, I decided to add a few more trinkets to my loot. Another hour and I would've gotten away with a fortune.

Mickey   But then Goofy turned on your machine and acciden-
tally caught you in your own trap!

Goofy   Gawrsh, Ben, I'm sorry we suspected you.

Ben   Is okay. Now you know for sure, Ben Ahrownd is
best of all the guides. I knew to walk in city was bad
luck...especially for Mr. Lurks!